Don't Speak of the Butterflies

sabrina johnson

Published by sabrina johnson, 2024.

*To Jenna
lots of love
sabrina draper x*

This is a work of fiction. Similarities to real people, places, or events are entirely coincidental.

DON'T SPEAK OF THE BUTTERFLIES

First edition. March 3, 2024.

Copyright © 2024 sabrina johnson.

ISBN: 979-8224208456

Written by sabrina johnson.

CHAPTER ONE

The Government machines clicked in and out of operation. How grace had died in them, a snared animal forever captured, forever soulless. They breathed out fresh air that morning.

The air outside so dead and thin, starved, a wretched corpse of a life short lived, no lover to visit her empty grave, it still belonged to the government, as did all death. She lay in waiting, singing with black flies.

Juliet had found herself there that morning, ticking away the minutes on the clock, ticking time into her dead life.

The machines shifted and came into operation again, their cold buttons clicking on.

She only noticed the noise when they switched off again.

She stubbed out the end of a hardly noticed cigarette on the cold stone floor, so dry.

She had committed the most illegal crime in the New World, she had attempted suicide. A deep black suicide, a scream to all the World.

She still bore the scars.

Something that night, something had chilled her soul, unspeakable terror, gorging on the death of all reality, death had called to her, the Angels in Heaven had sang to her soul, the song of escape, the songs of freedom.

She had cut deeper and deeper, then she had poisoned herself, the poison that had poisoned her favourite philosopher.

"I need to explain" she had thought

"I need to tell the World who I really am"

"I need to do this"

Oh how little she had to say.

She had slid into a long coma.

No one could switch off her life support machine as it was against the law, against all religion, against all reason.

Maybe modern medicine would save her one day, and after so long, by a beautiful miracle it had.

She hadn't wanted to come back, she had only wanted to sleep for eternity. To wash away all the bad dreams, her blood running on tomorrows headlines.

I awake to a pretty breeze in a neat fresh garden. My Husband walks out and hugs me.

"Hello darling how are you?" I say.

"Oh ok how are you"

"Happy." I say. "I never thought I would see you again."

"Oh I came back to you. The War is over and there is Peace on Earth. Dont worry the Government sorted it all out, I knew they would."

"So did I!" I hug him even tighter.

I am sitting in a meadow, sunlight enrapture of the Gods.

The Earth drinks from the sky charmed and the flowers spring forth enchanted.

I am reading The Song of Solomon.

"I am the rose of Sharon, and the lily of the valleys.

As the lily among thorns, so is my love among the daughters.

As the apple tree among the trees of the wood, so is my beloved among the sons.

I sit down under his shadow with great delight, and his fruit was sweet to my taste."

My Husband listens. I admire his beauty, his intuition.

His big brown eyes peer at me as I read.

They are but objects of the devil, so deep and serene.

They drink of my heart.

I read on.

He brought me to the banqueting house, and his banner over me was love.

Stay with me flagons, comfort me with apples: for I am sick with love.

His left hand hand is under my head, and his right hand doth embrace me.

I charge you, O ye daughters of Jerusalem, by the roes, and by the hinds of the field, that you stir not up,

nor awake my love, till he please.

The voice of my beloved! behold, he cometh leaping upon the mountains, skipping upon the hills.

My beloved is like a roe or a young hart: behold, he standeth behind our wall, he looketh forth at the windows,

showing himself through the lattice.

My beloved spake, and said unto me,

Rise up, my love, my fair one, and come away.

For, lo, the winter is past, the rain is over and gone;

The flowers appear on the Earth; the time of the singing of birds is come, and the voice of the turtle is heard in our land:

The fig tree putteth forth her green figs, and the vines with the tender grape give a good smell.

Arise, my love, my fair one, and come away.

O my dove, that art in the clefts of the rock, in the secret places of the stairs, let me see thy countenance, let me hear thy voice;

for sweet is thy voice, and thy countenance is comely.

Take us the foxes, the little foxes, that spoil the vines: for our vines have tender grapes.

My beloved is mine, and I am his: he feedeth among the lilies.

Until the day break, and the shadows flee away, turn, my beloved, and be thou like a roe or a young hart upon the mountains of Bether.

Now it is his turn, his voice sweet as Angels as he reads to me.

I love his drama, his literate beauty.

His voice ebbs and flows as waves crashing at the shore.

I listen.

DON'T SPEAK OF THE BUTTERFLIES

"O Love, be fed with apples while you may,
    And feel the sun and go in royal array,
    A smiling innocent on the heavenly causeway,
    Though in what listening horror for the cry
    That soars in outer blackness dismally,
    The dumb blind beast, the paranoiac fury:
    Be warm, enjoy the season, lift your head,
    Exquisite in the pulse of tainted blood,
    That shivering glory not to be despised.
    Take your delight in momentariness,
    Walk between dark and dark- a shining space
    With the grave's narrowness, though not its peace."

The picture before me starts to flicker as an old film ruined by acid.
    "How long have you been in the Machine?" I hear a voice say.
    Then the picture flickers even more.
    "What machine?" she asked.
    The lights flickered on and she stood only in a white room naked but for the stickers dotted around her body, holding down wires.
    "The Machine, " came a voice, "The Dream weaver."
    "You've been in a coma for twenty years, we've plugged you up to the machine so it wasnt such a shock when you came round. You don't have to stay in the machine you can always leave, but the machine will help you live your deepest desires. It is our beautiful dream weaver, our latest human invention it is going to change mankind for the better, our beautiful virtual reality machine. You don't have to stay on the machine.
    You can always leave, but the World is a lot different now than what your used to."
    "In what way?" came her trembling reply.

"Oh, you'll get used to it. There's a war on now, but the Government are going to sort it all out."

Then as the cold steel air machines clicked back off she didn't want to remember more.

She remembered the white room.

She must escape from this place, but to where. The whole Planet was at war.

Had the whole world gone crazy, for if it had, she gone crazy with it, or was she the only person in her life who thought the whole world had gone crazy.

She had thought long and hard about staying on the machine. Life on it was just perfect. What made it a lie?

She became uncomfortable in the pronounced silence and left the building to join the throngs of people outside.

The streets were heaving with rat throngs of aimless souls. there eyes as empty as their souls.

They knew not where they were going. They followed each other aimlessly as sheep.

Oh what did God hold for them any more.

Dead, died, broken.

What beauty they must in reality behold, for what is life, but a stage.

They had chosen to stay on the dream weaving machine.

She longed to stay on the dream weaver too, but a small part of her also longed for reality.

Like they said, the Government were going to sort it all out, then they wouldn't need the machine and everyone could get on with their lives.

I turn a corner and an expensive car pulls up. I get in.

"Where are you going on this beautiful day?" asks my driver.

"Would you like to go shopping and buy some new dresses or maybe out for breakfast. I know a nice wine bar. All your friends will be there."

Someone bumped into her violently and she came round again.

"Wanker!" he shouted, "Get back on the machine!"

A scruffy bearded vagabond.

"My fathers an M.P." she said smartly.

He looked at her as a rabbit caught in bright headlines, fear was in his eyes. Then he scurried away.

"My beautiful blue skies. My beautiful vision. Stay with me all of the time, my dream weaver of all my dreams. For what more could I ask. Mankind are such intelligent forces of nature."

Then she drifted off home through the grey metropolis ignoring the beggars and prostitutes on the way.

CHAPTER TWO

She awoke that morning crowded with dreams.

Her dreams broke through into the afternoon where she lay on her bed, still contemplating the horrors she had found there and the beauty of the dream weaver.

It had taken her home, poppies heavy with seed, had taken her deeper and deeper, where memories are kept, tripping on the water like a laughing girl.

Like something from a beautiful song she once remembered.

They had mingled serenely untill the passion of the dream weaver had held all her deepest fears.

What horrors could the human race develope. Surely she would not have bad dreams in the dream weaver, for all her dreams would only ignite her passions.

She had held a dying baby in her arms in her dream, but she knew she had never even had a baby.

She had been sterilized by the government. This was only for the best.

She had held the baby, comforted the baby.

Oh how she longed to hold a baby, but as she had dreamt she had looked deeper and deeper into the baby's face until it had become a

doll with a shrill mechanical scream.

It's eyes massive and brown, terrifyingly crying,

it's eyes as hopeful as a lover with an engagement ring.

She was as a child sent from hell.

She had dropped the baby on the ground and it's head had fallen from it's body,

she had desperately tried to put it back on in the hope that the baby would come back to life, but it's head only fell off again when

she picked up the doll.

She tried to put the dream out of her mind.

A teabag and some milk. tainted spoons and tainted cups, for her heart was tainted, tainted by this cage she had to live in, no escape.

Upstairs, number thirteen, been built long after they thought to build a number
thirteen was bad luck.

"It's all we have I'm afraid. The proletariats are getting violent because of our wealth."

So here she lived at tiny number thirteen. Caged like a wild animal caught.

She routed round her desk for a cigarette, then lit up, smoking in the warm chemical air, chemicals of all nature, chemicals Hitler had used to gas the Jews in the second World War.

Life was but an endless cigarette.

She switched on her small radio, a song sprang from it suddenly, lighting up the dull morning.

It sang
"The rose tattoo, the fingerprints I need from you....

Marlene watches from the wall, her mocking smile says it all....

But the only soldier now is me, I think its called my destiny that I am changing..."

Then it sang
"Today I am a small blue thing made of glass....

I am turning in your hand....

I am scattered..... she couldn't hear all the lyrics clearly

I am turning in your heart, small blue thing..."

She lit another cigarette, and watched the smoke swirl in a myriad of music across a beam of light through her window.

The flowers she had collected from the Government gardens had now died, fifty red roses, their leaves muted green and crisp, their petals a deep dried blood red, they had died unopened.

They had never been thrown away.

Like the rest of the rubbish in her flat.

She had collected so many useless objects, her sideboard and her table were heaving deep in bits of everything one didn't need. And so the roses stayed.

They were quite arty she had thought, she might paint them and name them 'Love is blind'

But she would never find the time. She opened one, it fell apart all over the table, it was left lying there.

She remembered the song.

"Today I am a small blue thing made of china made of glass... I am turning in your hand... I am cold against your skin.."

She felt like a small blue thing made of china.. made of glass.

So small, so blue, she watched the smoke swirl like a twisting dragon breathing fire.

She was sure her lungs were black as a corpse, wretched as the state of the new world hospitals. It would probably bring on an early death, she knew this, but she just wanted to live for today.

Her depression deepened, her sadness serene as she turned the small blue thing around in her head...made of china....made of glass... I am turning in your heart.

She picked up her diary. It fell open at the last page on which she had written.

On it was written a poem, something she had scribbled down the night before.

It was named 'Valentine'

> Taste my tears
> They are the tears that run down my soul,

DON'T SPEAK OF THE BUTTERFLIES

Taste my words
They are the fears that burn in my soul
Be mine
Be my valentine
Each poem is a tear cried for you
Each word a thought of you
Salt stained words
Each word that I write for you
Cries out for the day it is read by you
Tears of honey
Be mine
Raindrops wet my tears
Tears wet my mind
Deep love slows to the rythms of life
Life slows to the running of tears on my heart
As does my heart
Hardened daylight
Falls on my mind
Slowing and filling
Every moment in time
I see the sunshine
Drowning my life in salt stained tears
In all its beauty
You consume the fire
You fill my soul with fire
Be mine
Be my valentine

She read it now, last night it seemed so real, so deep, so erotic, but now it was just another scribbled empty list on a piece of faded paper.

The ghost of herself had written it before, watching her tired life so lonely.

It puts one moment here, another over here, over here.

She put pen to paper, but nothing inspirational sprang to mind. Instead she wrote,

> "The War is not yet over, it is raging all around. When will it end. THe Government have promised it will end soon, but they've said that a million times now. I am beginning to think it will never be over. I'm not sure if I can stand this city any longer, this wretched life. Oh how I long to be back on the machine."

Then she dropped her pen on the crowded table and stared, just stared. into an empty void.

An empty void that now became crowded with images, the images she had tried so hard to keep from her mind, and for so long. She covered her face, but the images still came.

Her Father was talking to her quietly. "Tell anyone and I will kill myself. Is that what you want me to do kill myself."

"No Daddy she had cried, I won't tell." Her bruised throat kissed softly, then he was gone.

She tried to put the thoughts out of her mind. She replaced it with the dead flowers, with a song, anything that sprang to mind.....

Today I am a small blue thing, turning in your hand... made of china... made of glass... turning in your heart.

"Only reality, only reality," she chanted to herself as if it would break the spell and deliver her from all evil.

She had been here thousands of times before, she had visited endless psychiatrists, but they had all told her the same thing.

False memory syndrome.

She must dispell these images from her mind, for what mind did she possess that these things are living in there.

What demons did her soul possess.

Was she evil?

Her Father was a respectable man. Her Mother had died when she was five.

She had thought about jumping under a train to look after her Mother in Heaven, but her Father had told her Heaven didn't exist. Oh how he loved her so.

Mother hides the madness, stay Mother.

The smoke from another cigarrette swirled out of her window, a dragon chasing the last.

Then sleep came as a faded child.

Shadows. Deep shadows. She was running, running terrified running forever through endless doorways endless windows each one leading to the next never a way out.

Shadows. Deep shadows. When she awoke her room was shrouded in deep shadows, ghosts had filled its very depth, every corner, in which she turned to look.

She switched on the light.

Everything was as it was when she had fallen asleep.

Cold, crisp, clear, its lineated edges stricking her as reality.

It had become so late.

She looked out of her window, then she saw him, standing in the shadows, watching her. a man. A beautiful man, with a sad serene look in his pretty big brown eyes.

She moved away from her window, pretending not to notice him, but when she looked again he was gone.

She tried to put it out of her mind.

Then hunger took over her mind and she found a couple of pieces of cold pizza in her fridge. This just wasnt what she was used to, but it filled her stomache.

Then she switched on her shower, leaving the door ajar.

The light in her bathroom hadnt worked for months and she hadnt been able to find a shop that sold the right ones.

Her clothes slid off and she gasped a sigh of relief as the warm water hit her body, so clean, so beautiful as waves washing at the shore.

Her soft skin glistened wet in the half light as she slid the soap all over her skin, her breasts heavy as sleep.

She felt she was being watched.

This thought stayed with her for a while then ebbed away as she stepped out of the water, switching off the shower, and then silence.

She found her dressing gown in the bedroom and once dry threw it around her naked body.

Soft as a lamb in spring, beautiful as sweet innocence.

Would she ever sleep for she had slept all day, then the Government medication took her.

She dreams such sweet dreams. She dreams she is on the dream weaver.

Then from Heaven flies an Angel. His beauty unmatched in all the skies.

His slight hands sliding all over her dripping wet body, down deeper, deeper, deeper, a symphony so blue, on a rainbows edge, as waves washing against the shore,

Burying her deep in Angels tears, deep in the flowers of the devil, deep in love so as all the world turns with them,

Washing away her tears, washing away time,

Buried deep in her heart,

buried deep in her.

Her orgasm, beautiful as the feigning of sweet innocence.

CHAPTER THREE

She weaved through the undergrowth of the metropolis, dirty children ran screaming past her, an old woman smiled at her, her face ragged as a rock deep in make up.

As she passed she spotted an old red dog tied to a post, its eyes deep and sad, looked at her as if he knew her, she felt she knew him too for a second. She moved past.

A beautiful prostitute stared at her as she moved past, her eyes deep green as the grass fighting for air, fighting for life, growing wild through the deep cracks in the paving slabs.

An old man sang to his friend as he sat outside a small dirty cafe on a small chair drinking his tea. The old mans tune as old as his heart.

She walked on the buildings so old and deep in dirt from the cars which intermittently came crashing past.

The windows huge, most of them adorned with old greying curtains. Like big windows to the soul. What life must have gone on through them, she daren't look.

Oh how she hated this souless place, but in it she felt somehow free, lawless, alive.

The beautiful prostitute came to mind again, her eyes deep green, she put it out of her mind.

She buttoned her coat against the cruel wind, she never remembered the weather being this wet and cold in the summer.

The last thing she could recall about the weather was a heatwave every summer.

Then out of the corner of her eye she caught, driving past her, the beautiful man she had seen outside of her window the night before.

She hurried on then as she turned a corner she saw a car had stopped in front of her.

It was him again only this time he was masturbating, his hands thrashing down hard, and then the beautiful white come came flowing out of the end of his penis.

Her stomache flipped and then he drove off.

Who was he?

Would she ever see him again.

Was he following her.

She shivered.

Her final destination, the old train station.

Where was she going, she hadn't known, anywhere, anywhere that was not the cold cage of what was now her home.

She arrived.

Then she saw the beautiful man standing there on the platform, a book open in front of him.

His voice was barely audible above the noise of the buzzing crowd, but she could hear him quite clearly as he read.

Oh how he embellished the drama. She loved the sheer poetic beauty of his lyrical language.

"What else could we do, for the doors were guarded,
What else could we do, for they had imprisoned us,
What else could we do, for the streets were forbidden us,
What else could we do, for the town was asleep?
What else could we do, for she hungered and thirsted,
What else could we do, for we were defenceless,
What else could we do, for night had descended,
What else could we do, for we were in love?"

She stood and stared.

His voice ebbed and flowed as waves crashing against the shore.

I see red

The red of the twilight

The red of the half life

The red of the blood

DON'T SPEAK OF THE BUTTERFLIES

Cursing through my veins
The red of your embrace
The red of your stockings
Trimmed with lace
Did I see red in your face?
The red of my roses
Inadvertant poses
I see blue
The blue that taints the sky
The blue of you and I
The blue that melts the twilight
Blue scars of daylight lost
I see a rainbow melt into the night
Fill each shadow lost with light
Each sigh each breath
The colour of death
Blue against your soul
Red against your legs
Deepens with red until
The death of the dawn

Then he said "Stay off the machine"
    Then he whispered "Do you want me to rape you?"
    As she turned away then turned to look again the platform was empty and he was gone.

CHAPTER FOUR

Butterflies melted her heart, she could not discern the truth, but what truth there was in greiving. Oh, how there ever was for what seemed like ever more. she knew she would never see him again, for why would he want to see her again, magic never existed in her world that she ever knew of, only on the dream weaver machine.

But on the dreamweaver she was happily married and the story had only just started.

Was this her story though in this dungeon of life, a saphire glinting in the mud, ready to be found, or had he come to destroy all her dreams and warn her away from the machine? And why the hell should she listen, for she was a grown woman with a mind of her own.

Who the hell was he. Surely anyone doubting the Government was completely insane, wondrous though he had seemed, caught her at an opportune moment, stalking the life out of her, though he was. Why the hell should she listen to an insane stalker that was paranoid of the bloody Government.

She had awoke that morning full of burning dreams, question after question, face after face, that longed to be his to her heart. To her heart had cried a song, but as she awoke she could not remember or sing it only echo, till she came around reasonably, the deepest sorrow to her heart.

"Complete bloody stranger!" she remarked as she looked in the mirror.

"If only I had the money for some plastic bloody surgery. I mean who the bloody hell wants me at my age," Juliet asked the mirror questioningly. "But on the dreamweaver Juliet the World is your oyster, you are young and beautiful, in fact Juliet you are anyone you want to be, you will always be loved." Her eyes filled with a flash of uncertainty, which she caught as she looked away from the mirror.

This act sort of reminded her of a scene from a fairytale where the wicked stepmother asked the mirror, "Mirror mirror on the wall, who is the most beautiful of them all?" The mirror had replied that it wasn't her it was Snow White. Yes, that's what it had been called Snow White, she remembered now.

Snow White, with skin as fair as snow and lips as red as blood.

She covered her lips in blood red lipstick, no still not the fairest of them all, oh who would ever want her.

Anyway Snow White was cast out into the woods by her wicked stepmother, she quickly rubbed of the red lipstick as she looked in the mirror a glint of uncertainty in her eyes that this wasn't bad luck.

My Father loves me she said to herself, then as she washed her face the tears only mingled with the soap and water and as she dried her face she thought her eyes not too red to walk the streets.

As daylight broke birds sang a beautiful chorus of lovesongs. The sky echoed purple blue against her soul. She felt a faint glimmer of hope and she knew this would be a perfect day for the dreamweaving machine. The chilly air bit into her lips where she had rubbed at the red lipstick. Her mouth still tasted of coffee, she had actually been able to afford to buy coffee yesterday and this reminded her of a film she had once seen when she was twelve. Coffee and lipstick, a luxury. She hurried on, onwards each step closer to her new life on the machine.

"Where have you been?" asks my Husband imploringly, "I have waited all day for you to come back, I have missed you honey."

"Oh, nowhere, just shopping," I shoot at him the uncertain reply, for I remember the beautiful man and feel a touch guilty. In truth I don't know where the hell I have been, but I know I would never have an affair on him, he's not real though although in a moment I know he is as real as the daylight.

The beautiful man fades from my mind quickly, oh where could he be, but then he is gone.

"Honey, bought you a present," I say.

I hold out my hand and as I open it he sees there in my palm is a small blue thing.

"A chrystal, for me honey?" he smiles. "Your so clever, thats so beautiful! Does it hold energy and all that sort of stuff?"

"Oh yes I reply, this chrystal holds the energy from the dawn of my soul, don't ever lose it."

He kisses me deeply, sorrow into joy, mending all the world in my heart.

As I awake the computers were buzzing.

The dreamweaver seemed to be having problems and Juliet tried to close her eyes again, but the man shouted for her to get bloody off it.

"I'm so sorry," he said after he had calmed down, but that seems to be all for today, maybe you should come back tomorrow when we've got it online and working again properly.

Juliet discovered her complimentary coffee was still there and went to finish it off. The man shouted for her to leave it there, and she put it down quickly and shuffled of to put on her clothes.

Did nothing ever bloody work these days.

"Where have you been?"

Juliet swung around quickly in shock to see where the voice had come from. As she turned she saw it was the beautiful man again.

"Oh," cried Juliet, she looked as startled and taken unawares as a rabbit caught in headlights.

She remembered her husband on the dreamweaver machine and when the words "Oh, just shopping!" shot out of her mouth she was more surprised than he looked.

"Me too," replied the man, "And I bought you a beautiful present."

"Oh, what?" asked Juliet surprised.

He held out his hand and Juliet held out hers, she was unsure but the butterflies fired her fear into action and then there in her palm lay her present.

It was a small blue thing....

She shot a look of fear and longing at the man as he slowly walked away and then disapeared around a corner, she longed to follow, but she thought it rude, then the black butterflies took over and drove her slightly mad.

But he was so real, and so was the small blue thing.

Juliet hummed a tune to herself all the way home, ignoring the beggars and prostitutes on the way.

It rained for the rest of the day. Juliets hopes washed and faded out as she watched raindrops slide down her dirty window.

the rain fell like a never ending flow of acid tears. She looked at the small blue thing in her hand, it reminded her of a raindrop. Or maybe a tear.

Her tears began to flow alike raindrops and as the thunder crashed down outside one tear fell onto the small blue thing. It lit up like a dewy diamond and for a second and reminded Juliet of the stone from an engagement ring, this made her cry more. Then she was sure she saw the beautiful man for a split second standing in the pouring acid rush of a million tears, then he was gone....

She must get back on the machine, she thought.

CHAPTER FIVE

I am talking avidly to my husband, "Love on the underground."

His eyes flash playfully as he replies in a flash, "Seeks to destroy all that I am."

I look down, "The black suicide."

He touches my face, "Of a broken hearted man."

I wince, "Chained."

He laughs, "Garbage of the heart."

I feel my face light up, "Oil painting of the soul."

He replies, "Shamanic visions."

And so it goes on he replies then I reply back, one line each, it flows and flows as water through a valley.

"Trance is so old."

"Ravers in graves."

Ad libbed till we think in our graves.

"Transmitting your pain."

"Alternative comedians."

"Painting for slaves."

"Government blues."

"Breakfast at tiffanies."

"Tramps in my shoes."

"Gurus in blues."

"Old as the soul."

"Ravers now sold."

"Shoestring goals."

"Banksy in destiny."

"Arrested my heart."

"Fine as the times."

"Trendy simple simon says."

"Hotel California."

"Pink walls so small."
"Publish a list."
"Alice's mirror."
"Roundabout horror."
"Looking glass fame."
"Lost on the underground."
"Edit in pain."
"Goals of the soul."
"Punished and old."
"Rock and roll radio."
"managers adverts."
"Blues amalgamation."
"Distortion on pedals."
"sold for a soul."
"solid as fame."
"Water blues."
"Judge me not."
"For do I not bleed."
"All the Worlds a stage."
"Third time age."
"May's virginity."
"Trendy as slaves."
"Celestial names."
"God give me strength."
"For needless sowing my heart."
"Rasberries of old."
"Now on a cart."
"Orphans."
"Universal soldier."
"Wonderland."
"Create, generate, soar and..."
"Fly."

"Illuminate."
"Fire."
"Firefly."
"Destiny."
"Evervescent."
"Blue soul song."
"Blossoming of the soul."
"Generate."
"Scarlet and..."
"Black roses."
"Illuminate butterflies."
"Rainbows reflect."
"Zen."
"Equations."
"Illuminates."
"Forest flowers."
"Blossoming into lovers..."
"Hearts."
"Cupid arrows."
"Shooting stars."
"Blooming into daylight."
"Cool as oceans."
"Chrystal blue."
"Mythical soul songs."
"Swim through."
"Lovers oceans."
"To the river."
"Cries harps."
"Choir of Angels."
"Footsteps in the sand."
"Of time memorial."
"Poppies symphony."

"Green flowers."
"Towers fall."
"celestial calls."
"sing a new song."
"Snowdrops."
"Chrystals."
"Small blue thing..."
"Scattering scarlet ribbons."
"Around your heart."
"Sewing the seeds of Angel hearts."
He lowers his eyelids and looks deeply into my eyes and says, "Into you, into daylight."
I reply, "For a furnace of the sun, to fire your eyes."
Lips red run.
In between my legs.
Open heart.
To swallow all,
That is shining.
Dawn of a golden era.
Until all is night.
Black as my soul.
He breathes, "Free as a bird."
He undoes my black ribbons,
Scattered across,
Tomorrows,
Rose gardens.
Brambles catch at my black ribbons.
"Into me,
are you."
"Unto you I am."
I sigh, "You will scatter white ribbons,

flowingly
all tangled up
until you
dance upon me."

Streaming.
Screaming,
into music.
Mozart,
Turning in his grave.
I cry, "For you write the story of my heart."
Until dawn.
Red and Purple.
"For you write
the watercolours
of a dozen red roses," he sighs.
Across the morning.
All,
Tangled up,
Until,
You,
Scatter white ribbons,
Across my skin.
Scarlet as the blood of roses that flows from within.

CHAPTER SIX

The sky was melting slowly into a dark blue as she arrived home.

She could not find her key, and then after a while she found it and the lock gave a satisfying click open. She had tydied her small flat from top to bottom. She knew she would never have any visitors, but hope had come in a faded way for a few tiny hours.

She made herself a cup of coffee then sat down at the small table in her kitchen. She switched on the small black and white television in her kitchen. The war raged, unabated, fire lit up her darkened kitchen. Juliet switched it off quickly then shivered, a chill running through her soul, black as the ace of spades.

Opening her diary, with a heavy heart, Juliet winced as the page fell open on the last page she had written on.

> 'The War is not yet over. It is raging all around. When will it...' She flipped over the page onto the next page. It was clean and white as snow in sunlight. Juliet thought deeply for a minute or two, then started to write slowly...

'With what to do later,
I paint pictures,

  of Heavens and skies,

I draw flowers,

  and sweet lullabies.

I see things that set

  the heavens afire,
  but all the brushes of the skies,

will not colour my palette, only fill my mind,
with what to do later.

Then a poem comes to mind,

with what to do later.'

The results she found quite pleasing as she read it out loudly and passionately, then the window slammed shut loudly. She jumped up to close it properly, but spotted the beautiful man outside in the rain. She opened the window wide and stuck her head out the window.
He started to speak...

"Midnight cats,
the issues,
crawl out of bins,
scream in the starlight,"

His voice rose and dropped passionately and playfully. He was but an actor on this dark stage.

"play and hide,

lovers lovesongs,

fly into the face of the sun,

scarlet works,

blushing like children,

timeless in our hearts,

sing a new song,

melodies of laughter,

ring out,

in the cold midnight,

today

will we live for,

black and white,

cold hearted,

sown of sight,

gospel choirs

crawl out of the night,

strings of hearts,

sweet necklaces,

chains of flowers,

weeds blossom

dandelians ruined

faded pictures,

actors loom,

tapestries,

DON'T SPEAK OF THE BUTTERFLIES

threads,

webs,

one night stands,

of glory,

divination,

of our pockets,

to hold the posies,

roses,

bloom purple and gold,

painting time,

into daylight,

savage our screens,

rivers fade into dreams,

drinking bleach,

in our hearts,

tears passing,

lovers death darts,

cold as the soul,

alcohol goals,

diamonds cut,

glittering old,

cats eyes,

drive in a straight line,

line after line,

scrubbing

back street toilets,

of walls,

where prophets,

grow old.

Fag ash eyes,

holes in our souls,

purple rain,

it's such a shame,

our friendship had to end,

sinderella,

lost,

DON'T SPEAK OF THE BUTTERFLIES

teletubbies dreams,

sun city,

surfing,

technicolour dreams,

print on demand,

goals old.

Stares,

spit,

midnight,

rare roses,

black as night,

strings of hearts,

walk into light,

shining in our eyes,

the memories of a past,

life,

lies,

sold,

empty,

blowing through windows,

the doorways of the soul."

Then he was gone.

Juliet panicked.

She ran out of her front door, grabbing her keys on the way and slamming the door behind her. She ran blindly into the rain, the rain mingling with her tears.

"Don't go!" she yelled into the darkness.

She ran through the god forsaken streets untill suddenly someone jumped on her and she crashed to the ground.

"You wont get away with this!" screamed Juliet, her voice ringing through the cold empty streets.

"All dressed up and nowhere to go." the beautiful man whispered in her ear.

"You wont get away with this!" gasped Juliet.

"Well do you want it or not?" he laughed.

"Yes." she said quietly.

He ripped open the front of her dress

He spoke quietly and urgently.

"Art unfolds.

DON'T SPEAK OF THE BUTTERFLIES

I drew from my heart,

old, until cold,

climbing the walls,

art unfolds."

Her pink rosy knees bled into the cold grey pavement.

His lips trembled as he spoke...

"Climbing the walls,

of old songs,

scratched and tuneless,

tuning into deserts,

golden pyramids,

servants dead,

scraping graves,

out from gold,

we

as

a

nation,

talking

in

riddles

all for one

and one for all,

hiding in bunkers,

lovelorn,

lover."

He kissed her face then her red lipstick smeared across his tightening grip.

His voice more urgent.

"Eyes sunken

to sail a thousand ships,

tell me never

your gold tresses,

forlorn on the pavement,

eyes, black,

raven in her soul,

eating my heart,

drawn from it,

all the passion,

until cold,

He pulled at her hair, she sreamed. He carried on...

chocking

on my soul

breaking bread,

feeding

the

millions

a crumb

for posterity,

Jesus love,

now dead

now

old

"Do you love me?" He shouted at her, Juliet sobbed.

He whispered endlessly...

"I drew from my heart,

all the passion,

to make a new start,

counting teardrops,

counting pennies,

choking on

children's hearts

lost

dinner

money,

fine wines

of Jesus,

the last supper

in for a penny,

in for a pound,

of flesh,

alas poor friend,

fiends

end

in my heart

I cannot

hold

all loves lost

any longer,

profound,

dead,

sinking ships

battleships

coming of age

old newspaper fame

in a hospital

with

no medicine

crying blood

to the devil.

He asks her again, whispering, "Do you love me?"

He cries...

"My lover,

lies

in a

bed of forget me nots,

a blue

angel

ties

my

heart

into a string of hope."

"Yes!" sobbed Juliet, "Yes, I love you!"

Then he came inside her enough come for a thousand government babies that would never be.

He held her as she cried and whispered to her "If you love me you'll stay of the machine."

CHAPTER SEVEN

I am standing, staring at my beautiful husband. He stands behind a wire fence. His eyes hold in each a crystalline drop of sorrow. I am about to ask him why, as if I do not already know, then he starts to speak, sadly but clearly...

"Houses boarded,

rent applauded,

doom mongerers in the light.

I failed at school,

test papers and tools,

teaching the unlearned lessons,

of a thousand years,

driving through my heart,

in a thousand tears,

all sail across these egyptian nights,

kids applauded

for jordan's fame,

clothes red,

teachers dead,

you sang to me

through the school gates,

your mum

couldn't afford the rates

of test papers,

and I never saw you again.

Marks and spencers exploded

onto the headlines.

In our hearts

we felt the final

cut.

Advertising doom,

in rented

dirty rooms,

the teachers cruel,

in rented,

dirty,

rooms.

DON'T SPEAK OF THE BUTTERFLIES

Advertising doom,

war mongerers,

fumes,

in our hearts,

we

felt

the final cut.

I carried your books,

old fashioned soot,

and

swept

our hearts

away,

in the dustbins,

of Liverpool.

Charming lights,

go out in

the old school.

Where were our Fathers,

fighting in foriegn fields,

over land

that didn't

belong to us,

poppies creeping

through daisy chains,

in fields of

red,

blue bells

dead,

crooked and gold,

selling to

our souls,

mirrored in ashes,

and fumes,

snow white and

doomed,

DON'T SPEAK OF THE BUTTERFLIES

lips as red

as old foghorns,

crying

daylight

to

all

out of sight

and sundry

churches

of castles

in

the

air

glowing pennies

from our pockets,

to kill the old,

in fields red,

and sold,

creeping through cracks,

of offices,

broken

backs

and white

walls,

advertising,

all that

is to come,

in markets,

sold,

small.

Growing old,

carrying your books,

from

the schoolyard

onto my childrens

graves,

in

its

finest

glowing

manifestos

of

jealous

old age pensioners

leaving their inheretance

of crumbs."

I now speak sadly...

"I fastened a red piece of card

to my dress,

in memory

of

the human race,

who were losing

all face,

in the eyes of God,

now

dead

in his

cow shed

buckling under

the pressure

and floating

away

in our hearts where faith

ends

not starts.

New born babies cries,

tears

sold

passions

overflowed

on

DON'T SPEAK OF THE BUTTERFLIES

to our screens sold

I want

your daughter

her name

is

old

she's a

human

baby."

I wave goodbye with a heavy heart.

The picture melts as acid melting into my heart.

CHAPTER EIGHT

"I've heard your a spy." said Juliet to him that evening. He had caught up with her on the way home.

"We spend all week waiting for the weekend, all day for the night and all night for the day, we waist all our lives just waiting." he said back.

> Juliet unlocked her front door and let him in, her little flat now full of flowers from the Government gardens, it smelled so sweet.

"I've heard the government are sending out human looking robots to spy on people!" she laughed.

"I've heard you've been naughty." he said as he undid her red dress.

"My beautiful robot." whispered Juliet as she stood naked, the cool evening whispering through the curtains.

> "My beautiful robot,
>
> dancing alone,
>
> mathematics steal our minds."
>
> He whispers back, "Flowers discern our hearts.
>
> Shapes so shifting,
>
> until you say,
>
> say all those things you kept with you,
>
> on a rainy day."
>
> Juliet trembled and shivered.

DON'T SPEAK OF THE BUTTERFLIES

She said quietly, "The clock that ticks,

The hour that binds,

unseen, undone,

working on our minds,

the revolution ticks away,

all sown up,

all gone away,

in my lovers heart,

a making of destiny,

timeless in our eyes."

He cried as he slid in and out of her wet insides, "You come to me,

trembling as a clockwork flower,

upon the tide of the revolution,

comes your beauty,

so disdainful,

so erotic,

so unreal.

My broken mechanical heart,

cries out to see deep within you,

do you love me,

I say yes,

A soul that holds all

the power of nature,

springs forth,

all that a curse

carries with it.

Am I cursed.

Yes I say,

I am but a human being."

Juliet cries, "The curse of the machines,

the power of God,

brought you to me,

my beautiful robot,

am I cursed,

the curse of the songs

of love dance around my heart,

cursed until I die,

entwined, enraptured by

your soul, your words,

your orgasms,

hold a deep curse of slavery,

to you I am bound eternaly,

into your mouth, into your heart,

steel cold and beautiful,

grows all the flowers of my soul,

feeling their roots deep for cold steel,

to water my life with your tears."

As she orgasms deeply he comes inside her and she cries, "I belong to you!"

He says quietly, "I know what it's like to be dead,

I know what it's like to be sad."

Juliet writes in her diary that evening "Oh, the lies, still I miss you, sometimes I feel like dying."

Then on the next page she writes:

'The army are closing in, the revolution is lost, the Government will always win. They have all the technology and all the robot brain power. They have taken all the geniuses and recorded their

personalities and turned them into government robots, all is lost. The rain is getting worse,

all is lost.'

CHAPTER NINE

"You haven't been on that machine again have you?" suddenly asked the man as Juliet turned the corner straight into him.

"No, of course not." she replied angrily.

"Well have you!" he screamed at her as he shook her.

"What's it got to do with you!" she screamed back. "I'll do what I want, your not my keeper!"

"The machine is dangerous, you need to stay away from it, it will kill you!" he shouted into her face imploringly.

She shook herself away from his grip. "Your so fucking paranoid!" she snapped at him. "The machine is everything I wanted, everything is perfect on the machine, anyway it's not even real, what could be so damn dangerous?"

He calmed down and said to her quietly and imploringly as he took her into a doorway "Juliet, it's not a virtual reality machine, it watches lost memories. That coffee they give you, it brings back memories that have been lost due to pain. It unrepresses them. The Government only want to spy on you and find out what you have been doing. don't you understand, you need to stay away from it."

"But that man," she sobbed "He's really my husband, what happened to him, why did it hurt!"

The man stopped a sad look in his big eyes, "He died in a war, that's the truth ok, now you have it."

He went to put his arms around her but she broke away sobbing and ran down the empty wet street.

When she arrived home she threw herself on her bed, covered in rain, and sobbed until the cold dull daylight.

CHAPTER TEN

When Juliet awoke in the middle of the cold dark night, she could hear singing floating through her open window. She went to the window, he was stood in the street singing...

"When I find myself in times of trouble,

> Mother Mary comes to me,
> speaking words of wisdom,
> let it be,
> let it be, let it be, let it be let it be..."
> He had a beautiful voice.

"Not you again!" she said morbidly, and slammed the window shut.
Juliet could hear him saying from the other side of the window,
"We wait all day for night, and all night for day, we waste the whole of our lives waiting."
Then he said sadly " I know what it's like to be dead, I know what it's like to be sad."
Juliet just stood staring out of the window, her eyes filling with dewy tears.
Then he said, "My lover lies in a bed of forget me nots, a blue angel ties my heart in a string of hope."
She opened the window and gasped into the rain "I love you." her breath like a ghost.
She ran to the front door and as she opened the door she threw her arms around him crying. She dragged him up the stairs.
"Mother Mary?" she asked sweetly. "I don't believe in God."
"Do you want God?" he asked.
"No I don't want God." she replied seriously, "You are my God."
"And you my servant." he replied.

"What I want to know," he said laughing, as he slid of her stockings, "Is if your going to be faithful." Then he tied her to a chair with them.

She closed her eyes and said nervously, "He loves me, he loves me not, he loves me, he loves me not..."

He slid a daisy between her breasts, he had found it in a bunch of Government flowers.

She opened her eyes.

"I will crush you like a flower." he said seriously.

"I feel the warmth of revenge, to have or to have not."

"Is it a crime that I want you.

> Life is like a beautiful hell when your there,
> an empty hell when your not."

"Your the juices of a thousand red poppies to make me lovesick, so vile and beautiful, filled with your lies."

He whispered "Your beautiful throat." as he touched her throat, her head back, her eyes closed.

"Your divine smile,

> etched into my nightmares,
> deep sodden and wet,
> pale velvet inside my soul,"

He shoots across the pale soft wilderness.

"and find you lying silent in my dreams."

"The beauty of the slaves is they don't know they slaves."

Then he fucks her so violently it's as though he's raping her, she screams and screams all her orgasms violent too.

She was alone,
she felt empty now,
somehow betrayed.
On the carpet stared a stain,

when she had spilled her soul,
onto the deep velvet crushed rug.

CHAPTER ELEVEN

"Shall I sing you a blue soul song." laughed Juliet sweetly.
  "For if music be the soul of love then play on." he smiled.
  Juliet started to sing, a rhyme, a verse, a sing song melody. Her voice sweet and silken as the stars.
  "Should I begin, with no hesitation,

> should I risk it, can't resist it,
> vulnerability coming over me,
> and I'm feeling so weak,
> you were a part of me, just like a melody
> over and over,
>
> I lose control to each beat,
> your love is like candy, so sweet,
> you were a part of me, just like a melody,
> over and over,
>
> back when romance was a bore,
> each beat reminds me,
> all this time,
> dancing in rhyme,
> can you feel me?
> are you with me?
>
> I lose control to each beat,
> your love is like candy, so sweet,
> you were a part of me, just like a melody,
> over and over,
>
> I don't need nobody to make me over,
> this guise so hard to disguise,

DON'T SPEAK OF THE BUTTERFLIES

when he smiles his eyes light up,
see my world starts to fall,
here it is, the one you've been waiting for,
so unveil, unfold,

It's just me, here I stand,
slowly stripped."

Her last garment fell to the floor.

"Pale as white velvet." he whispered as he slipped his fingers inside her.
Then as he knelt at her feet he said "Juliet I adore you."
Pink as sweet velvet, soft and wet as dew.
All her splendours opened,
her face and heart it bloomed like a sweet flower.
he suspended every sense with his caresses,
the rain poured in through the open window,
christening them in tears,
her orgasm drank in the sun and shone like thunder.
And he stole her heart, and her life blood, as he pushed up deep inside her,
and she rippled like the deepest ocean, her breath deep as the storm,
the twilight stealing her beauty,
until all was darkness,
her screams echoing around the room,
chasing away all the sanity in him,
her cries seep sweetly into the night air,
feeling for the soulful blue of the midnight hour,
until dawn choruses of sweet love songs.
The dew of the morning trickling down the insides of her thighs.

CHAPTER TWELVE

That night the traffic was heavy outside her window. light intermittently beamed through her darkened window interrupting the still quiet air as she lay in his arms.

"The outer limits are underwater my love." he said quietly.

"I know." whispered Juliet.

Silence.

Stillness.

Then another car came crashing past, then another.

"We will have to drive all night." he said.

"You never told me you had a car." she replied.

"I never told you a lot of things." he said.

They dressed slowly and Juliet packed the few clothes she had into a bag.

All was quietly and slowly done, they packed all the blankets they could find.

Then another car came crashing past, then another.

"Is there any one you want to take?" he asked quietly.

"No." replied Juliet even more quietly.

They drove silently through the night, tears streaming down Juliets soft pale face.

Then they talked.

They talked all night.

He told her all about the Government institution he was brought up in and how he escaped when he was fourteen. He told her how they tried to use him as a weapon of war and how he had figured it out early on, before he was seven. She told him all about her childhood and her Mother dying when she was five and how she couldn't get anyone to believe her Father had raped her. He told her that he believed her and she cried again.

Then they stopped at last and carried on talking untill until dawn broke through glorious and beautiful.

Then through the wet beautiful green grass they climbed and climbed until they came upon an old circle of stones. The view was magnificent all captured in deep red and blue.

"This is a magical circle." he said.

"I know." gasped Juliet.

"I adore you." cried Juliet as she knelt at his feet.

"Pale as white velvet." she whispered, then her mouth full of pale velvet.

He cried into the dawn captured in red magnificent.

"Juliet, I love you too." he cried.

The rain poured down, christening them in tears.

As she stole his heart, his life blood, and the sun shone gloriously.

He gasped into the strange blue so sweet.

"Sweet as honey." breathed Juliet.

And the rain crashed down christening her breasts in tears where he had undone her dress.

They were both naked in the warm wet air, soft and sweet as Angels singing.

They made slow passionate love unaware of the World turning.

The rain running down their wet bodies.

As natural as the ocean to the shore, both crying tears of rain.

"The machine gave you to me, my clockwork flower." breathed Juliet

"Even the glow in your beautiful eyes looks human." she cried, "Your cold fingers tear at my heart, when you've taken me then will you kill me!" she cried. Juliet closed her eyes.

"I am human." he implored. "Only human. I have come back to you Juliet, it's me, can't you tell, i've had plastic surgery, it's me your husband."

She could not see the tears streaming down his face, the rain was becoming fierce.

He touched her mouth, "For your lips my love are as perishable as a sweet flower, drown you in my love, for nothing and no-one with touch you again, I'm here now. The chains across your heart undone. I escaped Juliet, they took me to war, they tried to use me as a weapon again, but I had to come back to you, I had to find you, I had to save you. You can't remember anything can you. They took you away and tortured you, all your memories lost, sweet and innocent, clean as the day you were born. Your soul is open, it shines from you." he thrashed in and out of her as waves washing against the shore.

"My soul stolen from your eyes as Angels that drink of celestial tears."

His tears poured onto her skin mingling with the rain.

"My Juliet, you were so young so wild and free, you will be once again."

Her wet hair wrapped around her angelic face.

"Did you like the morphine my love." he wept into her closed eyes.

Then she opened her eyes for a second and whispered, " I didn't even realise I had died." Then she went back to sleep and her breathing stopped.

He cried "So young and tender, the dead are tender, shall we kiss." he kissed her mouth gently.

"For you are all but a dying flower in a dying world, breathing it's last breath, where roses and lillies abound." The sea swirled around their bodies, waterlogged and drowning.

"They tortured you Juliet, after they killed our baby." he cried the tears of a thousand years.

The sky behind him lit up, a flash, a mushroom cloud.

"You shall die a flower opened." he said and a deep love rushed inside her.

Rain pours a deep song into the sea screaming wildly don't let it end.

That boy left longing and lonely in the rain.

Milton Keynes UK
Ingram Content Group UK Ltd.
UKHW010304070324
439018UK00001B/44